Chuck's Band

by Peggy Perry Anderson

— Green Light Readers —

Houghton Mifflin Harcourt
Boston New York

6/17
Kids
AND
ER

To Niece Janna and Nephew Tyler

The Library of Congress has cataloged the hardcover edition
as follows:
Anderson, Peggy Perry.
Chuck's band/by Peggy Perry Anderson.
p. cm.
"Walter Lorraine books."
Summary: Chuck and his barnyard friends form a band, but
they have trouble finding an instrument for Fat Cat Pat to play,
since all the cat wants to do is sleep all day.
[1. Bands—(Music) Fiction. 2. Domestic animals—Fiction.
3. Stories in rhyme.] I. Title.
2007021728
PZ8.3.A5484Chp 2008
[E]—dc22

ISBN: 978-0-618-96506-9 hardcover
ISBN: 978-0-544-92620-2 paper over board
ISBN: 978-0-544-92621-9 paperback

Manufactured in China
SCP 10 9 8 7 6 5 4 3 2 1
4500647233

This is Chuck.

3

To town he went.

He bought a
musical instrument.

Flo can hear Chuck's new banjo.

A mandolin is good for Flo.

"We want to play!"
bark Nip and Tuck.

Nip and Tuck hum and pluck.

"Wow!" says Sue.
"Wow, too!" says Lou.

11

Lou plays washtub. Thump, thump, thump!

Sue plays fiddle with a joyful jump!

Huck the workhorse
heard the song.

15

With a bass violin

he can play along.

"I hear music!" Duck Luck quacked.

The washboard raps
as Duck Luck taps.

They play together.
Hum, strum, pluck!

Now the chicken sings, "Cluck, cluck, cluck."

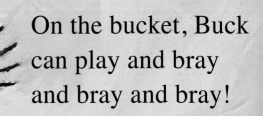

On the bucket, Buck
can play and bray
and bray and bray!

Fat Cat Pat has quite a pout.
Maybe she feels left out.

Did she want this?
Did she want that?

Nothing seems right for Fat Cat Pat.

What was that cat up to now?

Together they hum and strum and play
and tap and cluck and pluck and bray!
And Fat Cat Pat can sleep all day.